PUFFIN BOOKS

LIZZiE & LUCKY

The Mystery of the Stolen Treasure

... is the hugely popular au... ...r of a...
ad...ture books set in the modern day and key p...
of history. An animal advocate and dog-friend, Meg...
draws inspiration from her own adorable dogs Traffy,
Bella, Freya and Ellie.

Books by Megan Rix

THE GREAT FIRE DOGS

THE BOMBER DOG

THE GREAT ESCAPE

THE VICTORY DOGS

A SOLDIER'S FRIEND

THE RUNAWAYS

ECHO COME HOME

THE HERO PUP

THE PAW HOUSE

THE LOST WAR DOG

For younger readers

WINSTON AND THE MARMALADE CAT

EMMELINE AND THE PLUCKY PUP

FLORENCE AND THE MISCHIEVOUS KITTEN

ROSA AND THE DARING DOG

LIZZIE & LUCKY: THE MYSTERY OF THE MISSING PUPPIES

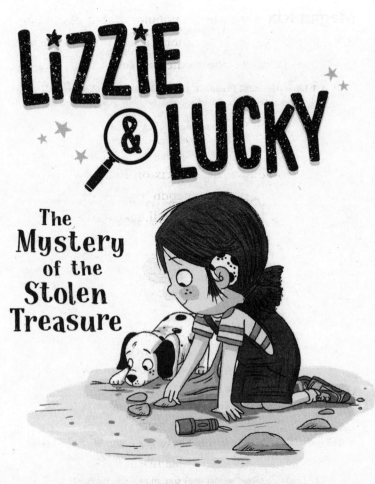

Lizzie & Lucky

The Mystery of the Stolen Treasure

Megan Rix

Illustrated by Tim Budgen

PUFFIN

PUFFIN BOOKS

UK | USA | Canada | Ireland | Australia
India | New Zealand | South Africa

Puffin is part of the Penguin Random House group of companies
whose addresses can be found at global.penguinrandomhouse.com.

www.penguin.co.uk
www.puffin.co.uk
www.ladybird.co.uk

First published 2021

001

Set in Bembo MT Std
Text design by Mandy Norman
Printed in Great Britain by Clays Ltd, Elcograf S.p.A.

The authorized representative in the EEA is Penguin Random House Ireland,
Morrison Chambers, 32 Nassau Street, Dublin D02 YH68

A CIP catalogue record for this book is available from the British Library

ISBN: 978–0–241–45553–1

All correspondence to:
Puffin Books
Penguin Random House Children's
8 Viaduct Gardens, London SW11 7BW

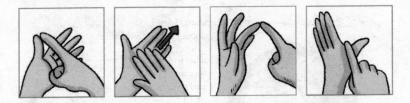

May your heart be your compass, and the stars guide you home.
May happiness always find you and your dreams come true.

– M.R.

To all the young adventurers and
mystery hunters, happy reading!

– T.B.

WHO'S WHO

Lizzie

Lucky

Ted

Tasha

CHAPTER

It was very early in the morning and it was **hot**, **hot**, **HOT**! Much too hot for eight-year-old detective Lizzie to sleep. She was sitting cross-legged on the multicoloured rug in her bedroom, surrounded by her mystery-solving equipment.

In her left hand she held a wooden clipboard; in her right hand she had a purple pen.

Lizzie chewed on the end of the pen as

she tried to decide what to take with her on holiday. What would be most helpful for mystery solving? The detectives in the stories she loved reading always had lots of useful things. Sometimes they had disguises so no one knew who they were. Sometimes they had lock picks – in case they found trapdoors leading to secret lairs hidden under rugs.

Lizzie wished she had a secret trapdoor hidden under her bedroom rug, but she didn't. What she did have was a detective dog.

Lucky, Lizzie's Dalmatian puppy, was lying on the rug next to her. Lucky's eyes were closed and her head was resting

on Lizzie's clue bag but Lizzie knew the puppy wasn't really asleep.

Lizzie looked down at Lucky and smiled. Lucky liked helping Lizzie solve mysteries – they were a great team.

Lizzie turned back to the equipment list she was writing. She liked making lists and had lots of them stuck on her noticeboard. Her favourite ones were decorated with glitter and stickers.

Before she'd met Lucky – or rather, rescued her from a thief! – Lizzie had made a list of 100 reasons why having a dog would be a really, really, really good idea. She'd been trying to persuade her parents to let her have one, but when Mum and Dad met Lucky they said they didn't need any more reasons – other than how much they all loved the puppy.

So far Lizzie's detective equipment list read:

1. White- and black-light TORCH – good for seeing in the dark and for reading invisible ink.

Lizzie and her friend Ted had been experimenting with different types of invisible ink. So far they'd tried lemon juice, onion juice, baking soda and vinegar. But there were many more combinations of ingredients to try too. Sometimes you had to wet the paper

to read the message and sometimes
you had to heat it up. But even better
than trying different ink recipes, Lizzie
liked using her black-light torch to read
them. It turned invisible-ink writing
purple.

She switched the torch on and off to
check the battery.

2. PHONE

Lizzie's phone had been very helpful in
her detective work so far. It had acted as
a silent, secret police communicator when
she and Lucky had rescued stolen puppies
a month ago.

3. Day- and night-vision BINOCULARS

These were brand new and a surprise present from Mrs Rose to say thank you for taking her hearing dog, Victor, out on lots of walks.

4. DETECTIVE GLOVES – for protecting hands and picking up clues.

5. DETECTIVE BAG

The animal rescue centre had given the bag to Lizzie and she always used it. They'd also given her and Lucky 'Animal Hero'

medals for finding the missing puppies, and both medals were hanging up on the wall.

6. MAGNIFYING GLASS

Sometimes a clue could be tiny and Lizzie didn't want to miss it!

7. Mum's old TWEEZERS and a packet of TISSUES – perfect for picking up tiny clues.

8. NOTEBOOK and PENCIL –  important for writing down clues and evidence, and making lists.

The next mystery could appear at any moment and Lizzie needed to be ready. It would probably be best to take all of her detective equipment with her, just in case.

Lucky sat up and her little black nose sniffed at the air. The smell of toasting toast wafted up the stairs and into Lizzie and Lucky's bedroom. Lizzie grinned and jumped up. The detective duo loved toast, so they ran down the stairs and into the kitchen to find Lizzie's mum and dad already there.

Dad raised an eyebrow when he saw Lizzie and Lucky, and Mum used sign language to tell Lizzie they'd been too hot to sleep.

Lizzie signed back that she and Lucky were too hot to sleep too.

When she and Lucky had gone to bed last night her mum's hair had been bright red but now it was purple! Mum had even plaited a little strand of Dad's beard and dyed that purple too.

Lizzie nodded. 'Nice,' she signed, pointing at her mum's hair and dad's beard.

Mum and Dad were sitting next to a pile of fake jewels, all ready to be put into Princess Joanna's crown. Princess Joanna of Scotland had been a real-life member of the royal family who had lived a long, long time ago and had been born deaf. The local Deaf theatre group were putting on a play about her, and Lizzie's mum and dad were in charge of the props.

'All done,' signed Dad, pointing at the fake jewels they'd made from coloured resin. Mum started buttering the toast while Lizzie got out the Marmite and Lucky wagged her tail.

'What we need is a nice cool sea breeze,' Dad signed, nodding his head. 'Maybe we should leave early and miss the traffic?'

Lizzie put her right fist in the palm of her left hand with the thumb stuck up, and then raised it quickly into the air with a grin. It was the sign for **'fantastic'**. She and Lucky crunched on a slice of toast.

Dad signed 'Text' and 'Ted' to Lizzie, who nodded and ran upstairs to grab her phone. Lucky ran after her.

By the time they came back downstairs with Lizzie's detective bag, her phone was flashing with a thumbs-up emoji from Ted.

Lucky tried to help by picking things

up from the floor as Lizzie, and her mum
and dad started racing round the house
grabbing swimming costumes, floaties
and towels. When she picked up her
four-legged, soft, yellow octopus toy and
brought it over to Lizzie, Lizzie put it in
her detective bag. They definitely needed
to take Lucky's favourite toy with them.

Last of all Lizzie put her new binoculars
and Lucky's red dog whistle round her
neck. She was teaching Lucky to come
straight back to her whenever she blew
the whistle, and Lucky wagged her tail
at the sight of it. The sound of the whistle
always meant cuddles, a play with one
of her toys or an extra tasty treat. It
didn't matter that Lizzie couldn't hear the

whistle – even hearing people weren't able to as it was a silent one – but Lucky and other dogs could, so long as they weren't too far away and the wind was blowing in the right direction.

'Ready?' signed Mum.

Lizzie nodded and put on Lucky's harness, then they all headed out to the car.

Ted, who lived opposite, was already waiting for them. He looked like he'd only just woken up. As well as a bag at his feet, he was holding a pair of flippers, an eye mask and a snorkel.

'**Wow!**' Lizzie signed, pointing to Ted's blue fin feet.

'Bet you can swim fast with those on,' signed Lizzie's dad.

Ted grinned and signed back, 'Yes, but they're not so easy to walk in!'

'Bye, Ted! Be good!' Ted's gran called out from an open upstairs window.

She waved at Lucky and Lizzie. 'Have fun!'

Lucky gave a woof and Lizzie held up both thumbs.

Ted noticed Lizzie's night-vision binoculars round her neck.

'New?' he signed, pointing at them.

Lizzie nodded, hoping she'd be able to use them soon.

'You never know when there might be a mystery to solve,' she signed back.

CHAPTER 2

Lucky jumped into the back of the car as soon as Lizzie opened the door. She loved going on car journeys with Lizzie because they always went somewhere exciting – not like the awful time before, when she'd been trapped in the bad man's van that smelt funny. Lizzie's car didn't smell funny. It smelt of toffee and adventures!

Lizzie and Ted climbed into the back of the car after her. Lizzie clipped Lucky's harness strap to the seat belt and the

puppy pressed her little
black nose to the window so she
didn't miss a thing as they set off.

At first they drove through the town
and Lucky only saw houses and other
cars. But when they went past the park
she saw a dog coming out and stood up
on the seat and wagged her tail.

★

Once they'd left town, Lizzie took out her
purple pen and clipboard with an animal-
spotting list on it.

'Sheep,' signed Lizzie, pointing to the
left.

She put a tick on the chart in the box
for sheep.

Lucky opened her mouth and barked,

and Lizzie laughed. 'Maybe Lucky thinks sheep are big, white, shaggy dogs to play with,' she signed to Ted. 'Cows,' said Ted, pointing to the right.

Lizzie put a tick in the box for cows.

She grinned at Ted as Lucky looked out of the window to see the cows.

'Even bigger dogs – black and white ones this time,' Ted said as he gave Lucky a stroke.

'Pony,' signed Lizzie a few minutes later, and she put a tick next to the horses and ponies box as the car drove on.

★

Half an hour later, Ted pointed excitedly into the distance. Lizzie and Lucky turned to see a line of blue far off on the horizon. **'The sea!'** signed Lizzie excitedly.

★

When the car finally stopped, Lucky was so eager to get out that she climbed straight over Ted's legs and got tangled up in her harness. As Lizzie and Ted were gently untangling her, Lucky sniffed at the air. It smelt different.

20

Salty.
Exciting!

They'd stopped outside a small wooden house with a big skull-and-crossbones pirate flag waving on a flagpole. Lizzie's dad pressed the car horn over and over.

'I gave that to them,' Dad signed, pointing at the flag.

'Looks good,' signed Mum.

Lizzie and Ted nodded and held up their thumbs.

★

A few minutes later, two old people came out of the house, still in their pyjamas, dressing-gowns and slippers. Their hair looked tufted up and messy. They rubbed at their sleepy eyes and then grinned

21

with delight when they saw who was at
their door.

'Early!' the old man signed.
'Good!' laughed the old
lady, holding her arms out to
Lizzie.

Lizzie threw her arms
round her gran and then
her grandad.

Lucky looked up at them for a stroke.

'You'll wake up the neighbours!' Gran signed at Dad as Grandad mimed Dad pressing the car horn over and over.

But Lizzie's dad only laughed and made the sign for **'don't care'** before giving them both a hug. 'If the neighbours were deaf like me then the sound wouldn't wake them!'

Grandad shook his head as he hugged Lizzie's mum and made the sign for **'too NOISY'** at the same time. Gran and Grandad weren't deaf like Lizzie and her mum and dad, but they could sign really well.

'That's why I like signing,' Ted signed, his hands moving fast and wide. If he'd been speaking he'd have been shouting, but he could sign as enthusiastically as he liked – with really big hand movements and gestures – and no one could hear him or tell him to be quiet!

'This is my friend, Ted,' Lizzie told them.

'Nice to meet you, Ted,' Grandad said.

'Is this the puppy you rescued?' Gran asked as she gave Lucky a stroke. Lucky liked being stroked very much. 'She's so sweet.'

Lizzie nodded and showed Gran the dog whistle. 'Lucky always comes back when I blow this. Only dogs can hear it.' Then she showed Gran her night-vision binoculars too.

'Very nice!' Gran said.

Lizzie looked across the sand with her new binoculars. The only other person she could see was a tall man with a big brown-and-white Newfoundland dog. When the man saw Lizzie and her family, he pulled down the red baseball cap he was wearing so it hid his face and strode off the other way.

Lizzie frowned. Why was he hurrying off like that? What was he doing on the

beach so early in the morning? And why
did he hide his face when he saw them?
She felt a shiver of excitement – it was
very suspicious.

Could it be a MYSTERY to solve?

Lucky seemed to be much more
interested in the big dog than she was in
the man. The dog looked over at Lucky
and the little Dalmatian barked and made
a play bow. The Newfoundland started
to trot over to her but then it stopped. Its
owner was walking away very fast, almost
jogging. He must have called the dog
without turning his head because it went
lolloping after him.

As the pair hurried away, a small scrap

of paper fell out of the man's pocket. It
was caught by the brisk sea wind and
came fluttering across the sand.

Lucky loved being helpful, so she
chased after the paper, caught it and
brought it back.

Lizzie unfolded it and frowned.

'What does it say?' Ted wanted to know.

Lizzie showed him the torn scrap of
paper.

'*Missing or stolen . . .*' was scrawled
across it.

'What does it mean?' Ted asked.

Lizzie didn't know but she wanted to
find out!

★

'Might just be part of a story,' Grandad

said when she showed it to him. 'There
are lots of writers around here. Almost
as many as beachcombers and treasure
hunters.'

'And there are lots of exciting stories
to be told, especially from the olden days
when there were pirates!' added Gran.

Lizzie put the scrap of paper in her
pocket. She didn't believe for one second
that it was part of a story the man was
writing. Not even a story about pirates!
Why would he tear it and then put it
in his pocket? There was more to this
than met the eye and she intended to

find out WHAT!

CHAPTER 3

Lucky looked up at Lizzie and wagged her tail. The sea breeze ruffled through her fur as she gazed curiously at the soft yellow sand and wavy blue water around her.

Lizzie and Ted started running across the beach towards the sea, so Lucky went racing after them and soon overtook the children. Running on the sand wasn't like running on grass or walking on the pavement. It was much better and more

exciting! Lucky barked
with joy.

When Lizzie and Ted reached
the sea they pulled off their shoes and
went paddling.

Lucky went bounding in after them,
but quickly began to hop about instead.
The water was very cold! She had a taste
of it and spat it out straight away – it had
a nasty salty taste.

★

Lizzie stared out to sea, where shiny black
rocks stuck up out of the waves. There
were more rocks on the sand, but next
to them green, brown and red seaweed

floated in tiny pools. Some of the rocks
were covered in shells.

'You can see shipwrecks all along this
stretch of the coast when the
tide's out,' Grandad told Lizzie
and Ted. Lizzie put
her binoculars up
to her eyes so that
she could see
further
out.

Grandad tapped her on the shoulder so she'd know he was still speaking.

'The sea can come in very fast, especially around the caves,' he said as Lizzie lip-read his words and nodded. 'Many people and ships have been trapped, and the landslide we had a few years ago made everything worse. A cave with a small entrance can turn out to be vast inside, and lead to other tunnels and caves. Or a cave with a huge entrance that looks interesting might lead to nowhere.'

Lizzie nodded again and held up one thumb. She thought the caves sounded a bit like puzzles to be solved. Nature puzzles – though dangerous ones.

As she looked at the caves through her binoculars, she spotted the man with the baseball cap and his big dog coming out of one of the entrances close to the path that led up to the cliffs. She thought about his torn paper in her pocket. '*Missing or stolen*' could mean something **VERY important!**

Lizzie waved her hands in the air to try and get the man's attention, but he didn't look over. He and his dog just headed into another cave.

Lizzie was now more certain that the scrap of paper *could* be a clue, no matter what anyone else said. She had a feeling inside that told her so.

Dad waved his hands in front of her

face to get her attention. 'When I was your age, me and my best friend Max were nearly trapped in a cave. It was scary. We used to explore the caves and go beachcombing every day. The best time to find things was after a storm. Sometimes we'd use a metal detector . . . until we weren't friends any more,' he signed. His shoulders drooped and he looked sad.

'Still got that metal detector in the garage,' Grandad said. 'Although it hasn't been used in years.'

'Why did you and Max stop being friends?' Lizzie signed to her dad. It was hard for her to imagine her dad falling out with anyone.

'He got jealous because I found an old

steel fire striker in the shape of an S,' Dad told her.

'What's a fire striker?' Ted asked him.

'It's what they used to make fire before we had matches and lighters.'

Lizzie frowned. 'How did it work?'

'Hundreds of years ago people had to strike a sharp stone on metal to start a fire. Must have taken ages,' Grandad said as Lizzie lip-read.

'I found the fire striker hidden under a rock in a rock pool. A crab ran over my fingers as I picked it up,' Dad remembered. 'Max wasn't there because he was in hospital having a cochlear implant fitted to help him hear more.'

Lizzie watched as Lucky sniffed at some seaweed that had been washed ashore and pawed at a tiny crab that scuttled out of it and away.

'Who did the fire striker belong to?' asked Ted.

'I don't know. But I hoped it had belonged to a pirate . . .

maybe even to **Sign Hand Stan**, the famous deaf pirate.' Dad made the sign for 'pirate' by putting his hand over one eye like a patch. 'He had a ship called the *Stormracer*.'

Lizzie made the sign for **'great'**. She hadn't ever heard of a deaf pirate before. (Although she assumed there must have been one because her dad was always signing, **'Everything a hearing person can do, a deaf person can do too!'**)

'Did Sign Hand Stan have hearing aids like me?' she asked.

Dad shook his head. 'Sign Hand Stan lived during the Golden Age of Piracy, which was a long, long time ago in the late sixteen hundreds and early seventeen hundreds. It was before hearing aids had been invented, so people had to improvise. Sometimes they'd use a cow or ram's horn as a hearing trumpet!'

'Sign Hand Stan used a big conch shell,' Grandad told Lizzie.

Lizzie looked over at the caves. The man and his dog were still there, now standing in front of a cave with a huge boulder blocking the entrance. The man had a notebook and seemed to be taking measurements.

Lucky was fascinated by the man's dog. Lizzie watched her puppy as Lucky sat down and then lay down, still looking in the Newfoundland's direction.

'What was the *Stormracer* like?' Ted signed.

'Big – with cannons on board,' Dad signed back. 'But Sign Hand Stan was a good captain who always looked after his crew. He made the other pirates eat lemons so they didn't get scurvy. Lots of sailors became deaf back then and we don't know whether Sign Hand Stan was born deaf or became deaf later on.'

'Why did sailors become deaf in the olden days?' Ted asked.

'Because of the loud cannons blasting in their ears, right next to them,' Grandad told him.

'Like your loud car horn blowing!' Ted signed, grinning at Dad.

Grandad shook his head and signed, **'much, much louder'**.

'They used boys called Powder Monkeys to load the cannons. It was a dangerous job. They had to bring the gunpowder up from the ship's hold to be put in the cannons.'

'And they had to be fast,' Dad added.

'Did they have girl Powder Monkeys too?' Lizzie wanted to know.

Grandad nodded. 'The largest ships back then had a hundred cannons on board so they needed a lot of Powder Monkeys to load them.'

'It sounds exciting,' Ted said.

Lizzie made the sign for 'dangerous' and Dad nodded.

'There were lots of ex-Powder Monkeys in Sign Hand Stan's pirate crew. Everyone used sign language on board his ship, although they weren't exactly the same signs as we use now,' Grandad added.

'The vowels back then were signed in the opposite order when they were fingerspelling,' Dad told Lizzie. 'Instead of touching your left thumb with your right index finger for the letter A, the way we do today, you would touch your little finger.'

Lizzie nodded. Fingerspelling letters was a slow way of signing. Mostly people used signs for words not letters – it was much quicker.

'But what happened to Sign Hand Stan and his ship?' Lizzie asked.

'Well, that's a mystery people have been

trying to solve for years,' Grandad
told her.

'His ship and all his crew disappeared
one dark and stormy night and were
never seen again,' signed Dad.

'Did his ship sink on the rocks?' Ted
asked.

'No one knows,' said Grandad.

Dad shrugged and shook his head.
'People have been searching for as long as
I can remember.'

'It's a mystery,' signed Ted, smiling at
Lizzie.

Lizzie smiled back because she
loved mysteries – and now she had

TWO to solve!

CHAPTER

There was a loud **squaWking** noise as soon as the front door to Gran and Grandad's house was opened – loud enough to make Lucky jump, and for Lizzie and her dad to hear it too.

'*What* was that?' said Ted.

'Iggy and Boo,' Lizzie signed to him.

'Who?' Ted frowned, raising one eyebrow as he looked at Lizzie.

Lizzie laughed and beckoned him towards the back door.

Iggy, the seven-
year-old, one-and-
a-half-metre-long
iguana, was relaxing in
her pool in the back
garden, but it wasn't
her that had squawked.
It was Boo, the elderly red, blue and
yellow parrot watching over Iggy from his
perch. He squawked and flapped his wings
every now and again as if he was her
bodyguard.

Lucky stayed next to Lizzie as they
went closer.

'Boo was my birthday pirate parrot when I was seven years old,' Dad signed to Ted.

'Did you get Boo when he was just a chick?' Ted signed back.

'No, he was already fully grown. Older than me,' Dad told him.

'Parrots can live for more than eighty years,' Lizzie signed.

Ted made the sign for **'wow'**. 'So how old is Boo?' he asked.

But no one knew that for sure.

'Sign Hand Stan had a parrot just like him. I wanted Boo to perch on my shoulder but he kept flying off!' Dad signed.

'Did you try to teach Boo to talk?' Ted asked excitedly.

Dad's nose wrinkled and he frowned. 'Talk? Why? Signing is better than talking.'

'Boo's never been a talker,' Grandad said. **'Woof, woof!'** squawked Boo – and Lucky jumped back fearfully.

Ted laughed and laughed as he gave Lucky a comforting stroke. 'I thought you said Boo couldn't talk?'

'I'm just as surprised as you,' Gran said, bringing out some fruit and vegetables for the pets' breakfasts. 'I've never known him do that before. He must like Lucky.'

Lizzie watched as Lucky bravely opened her mouth and barked at the parrot. 'Woof, woof, woof!'

'Woof, woof, woof!'

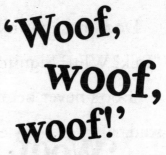

Boo barked back
at her.

Lucky ran and hid behind Lizzie's legs,
peeping out at the scary bird.

'I'd better be getting off to the Pirate
Museum,' Gran said. 'It's only open part-
time and I don't want to miss Tasha. She
loves my home-made seaweed chutney.'

Gran had made a special small clay
pot for the chutney. It looked a bit like
the pot she'd made for Lizzie to put her
pencils in last Christmas.

'You know, I gave the fire striker I

found to the Pirate Museum,' Dad told Lizzie. 'I had my picture in the local paper.' He pretended to be holding the fire striker and pulled a funny face. 'I was ten years old and famous already – for at least five minutes!'

'Can Lucky and I come to the museum too?' Lizzie signed to Gran. She wanted to have a look at Dad's fire striker – and see if she could find out more about the mystery of Sign Hand Stan.

'Anyone else want to come?' Gran asked.

Ted said he wanted to try and teach Boo some pirate words, Grandad wanted to finish some welding in his workshop and then see if he could get Dad's old

metal detector working, and Mum and
Dad wanted to go for a walk on the
beach.

'Just us, then,' Gran said.

Lucky looked hopeful and gave a little
wag of her tail as Lizzie went inside to
pick up her detecting equipment bag.

'You won't need that,' Gran said.

But Lizzie thought she might. You never
knew when a clue might turn up and
she wanted to be ready. She remembered
to add her night-vision
binoculars and Lucky's
whistle, and then put the
bag over her shoulder.

'Might as well pop this in there too,' Gran said, giving Lizzie a folded-up umbrella with a hook on the end, but Lizzie shook her head. The sky was a clear blue. They wouldn't be needing an umbrella.

'It's supposed to rain soon,' Gran told her. 'There's a storm forecast. The weather can change in an instant around here.'

Lizzie looked out doubtfully at the cloudless blue sky

again as she put the umbrella in her bag anyway.

'See you later,' signed Mum.

'Don't forget to take a photo of my fire striker!' signed Dad.

CHAPTER 5

The Pirate Museum wasn't very big, but it was easy to spot because there was a ship's figurehead of a unicorn sticking out of the wall, along with a skull-and-crossbones flag like the one Gran and Grandad had.

'All old ships used to have a wooden figurehead sticking out of the bow,' Gran told Lizzie. 'Sometimes they'd be made to

PIRATE MUSEUM

look like a king or queen, but other ships had things like dragons and snakes.'

'And unicorns,' signed Lizzie, pointing at the figurehead as they went in through the door.

Gran's friend Tasha was waiting for them by the entrance, wearing a pirate's outfit.

'Ahoy there, landlubbers!'

Tasha cried, waving a curved pirate's sword about.

Lizzie had seen a picture of a sword like it before and knew it was called a cutlass, but she didn't know what a landlubber was.

She looked down at Lucky, smiled and gave her furry head a stroke, but Tasha's grin disappeared when she saw the puppy. Her face frowned and she bit her bottom lip.

'I don't know if dogs are allowed inside any more,' she said nervously. 'The new museum owner is very strict.'

'Has someone bought the museum, then? That's good news, isn't it? I know it was short of money – you said it might have to close otherwise,' Gran said before handing Tasha the pot of home-made seaweed chutney.

Tasha nodded as she glanced behind her. 'His name's Mr Dobson. He was here just now but he's popped out. I'm not too sure about him yet – he keeps wanting to open up the glass cases and take a closer look at the exhibits. I tried to tell him some of the items are very fragile and he almost bit my head off. But it's his museum now, so I suppose he can do what he likes.'

'Would you rather we didn't come in with the puppy?' Gran asked, and Lizzie's heart sank.

But Tasha quickly shook her head and beckoned them further inside. 'Mr Dobson hasn't actually said dogs aren't welcome yet and there aren't any notices banning them. There's no one else in the museum at the moment, so your puppy can come off its lead if you like.'

Tasha didn't know any sign language and Lizzie was glad she had Gran with her to translate. Lip-reading was tiring and Tasha kept turning her face away, which made it impossible to see what she was saying.

Lucky's nose was busily sniffing along the carpet. Lizzie thought the museum must have lots of interesting smells.

She looked at the paintings of pirates on the walls and wondered if any of them were Sign Hand Stan.

Tasha stopped next to a portrait of a pirate named Anne Bonny. She had long red hair and was holding an axe. There was a plaque under the painting saying that Anne Bonny lived during the Golden Age of Piracy.

'That's when Sign Hand Stan was a pirate too, wasn't it?' Lizzie signed and Gran nodded.

Next to Anne Bonny was a painting of her best friend, Mary Read, another lady pirate. 'Were there lots of lady pirates?' Lizzie signed. Gran wasn't sure so she asked Tasha.

'Not as many as male pirates,' Tasha told her, 'but as you can see there were definitely some. There are more pictures ...'

But Lizzie had another question – a very important one. 'Were any of the lady pirates deaf like me?' she signed to Gran.

'Not that I know of,' Tasha said. 'Although of course there was Sign Hand Stan and his crew.'

Lizzie nodded. She was really looking forward to seeing his exhibit, but she wished Tasha knew of some deaf lady pirates. She was sure there must have been some. If there could be a deaf princess, like Princess Joanna, then there could definitely have been deaf lady pirates too.

Lucky sniffed at the carpet and sneezed.

Tasha stopped at an exhibit that showed lots of black-and-white skull-and-crossbones pirate flags, as well as some plain red ones.

'Original pirate flags were blood red,' she told Lizzie and Gran. 'The colour meant no mercy would be shown.'

'I prefer the skull-and-crossbones flags,' Gran signed as she spoke.

Lizzie nodded.

Tasha did too, but then frowned suddenly as she gazed more closely into the glass case. 'There's usually an ornate gold flag holder in the corner. It's for putting the flagpole into. Can you see it? It has a small green emerald embedded in the front.'

Lizzie pressed her nose to the glass. There were lots of flags and lots of cast-iron flagpole holders. There was even a bronze flag holder shaped like a bird, but she couldn't see anything gold with an emerald in it.

Tasha's brow furrowed. 'Perhaps Mr Dobson's moved it to another case. I suppose it would fit very nicely into the beachcomber exhibit. This particular flag holder was found in one of the caves on the beach, almost ten years ago now.'

Lucky trotted after them as they headed over to the beachcomber display, but the gold and emerald flag holder wasn't there either.

'Is this where Dad's fire striker was put too?' Lizzie signed, so Gran asked Tasha.

Tasha nodded, and pointed to the picture of Lizzie's dad, aged ten, holding a dark-coloured piece of metal in the shape of an S.

'He had such a cheeky grin,' smiled Gran.

'But where's the actual fire striker?' Lizzie asked.

They all peered through the glass but none of them could see it.

'That's very odd,' Tasha said, scratching her head. 'Your dad's find has been next to his picture for as long as I can remember. Where it can be is a mystery.'

Lucky looked up at the sound of the word 'mystery' and gave a wag of her tail. Lizzie clasped her detective bag. She knew she'd been right to bring it along.

Now she and Lucky had ANOTHER MYSTERY to solve!

CHAPTER 6

Lizzie thought that maybe Mr Dobson had moved Dad's fire striker to Sign Hand Stan's exhibit. She and Lucky headed over to have a look. Inside the display case were paintings and costumes, a skull-and-crossbones flag, a big gun called a blunderbuss and a real cutlass sword, like Tasha's pretend one that she sometimes waved about when she was talking.

Lizzie knew her dad would be very pleased and proud if his beachcomber find had been put into Sign Hand Stan's exhibit – the S shape could even stand for Stan! But although she looked at each object really carefully, there was no sign of the fire striker.

Lizzie saw Lucky scratching and sniffing at the door of an adjacent cleaning cupboard and beckoned the puppy back.

Fortunately Tasha didn't notice as she tapped Lizzie on the shoulder and pointed to a painting of the *Stormracer*. It's figurehead was a giant carved wooden hand.

'Sign Hand Stan is said to have painted that,' Tasha explained, as Lizzie lip-read. 'Although there's no signature, so we don't know for sure. These items were all donated to the museum anonymously. Some people even think they were given by the descendants of Sign Hand Stan himself.'

Tasha pointed to a portrait that was hanging next to the *Stormracer* painting. It was a picture of Sign Hand Stan. The pirate had long, wavy black hair that stretched down past his shoulders and a beard to match. Lizzie stared at it and thought that for all his wild pirateness, the artist had given Sign Hand Stan very kind and twinkly eyes.

'That portrait probably isn't exactly what Sign Hand Stan looked like. They didn't have cameras back then,' Tasha said.

Sign Hand Stan was wearing a brown three-cornered hat with gold trimming.

'That's called a tricorn hat,' Gran said, reading from the exhibit notes. 'They were so popular in the olden days that people wore them indoors and out.'

Lizzie grinned and pointed at the big, hooped, gold earrings Sign Hand Stan was wearing.

'Dad would like them,' she signed.

Gran laughed and nodded. 'Some pirates were very superstitious,' she read and signed to Lizzie. 'They believed the precious metal in earrings possessed magical powers.'

Lizzie made the sign for **'WOW'** and then spotted something else. 'What's that?' she asked, pointing at a yellowed sheet of paper with curly writing on it. The paper was on an easel in the centre of the display.

'Ah, now that's very interesting,' Tasha said. 'It's the *Stormracer*'s pirate code.'

'Pirate code?' Lizzie signed to Gran. She didn't know what that was.

Tasha nodded. 'Back in the Golden

Age, pirates had strict rules about how the crew should be treated. Captains had to be voted in by all the other pirates, and everyone was treated exactly the same.'

Lizzie held up both thumbs. She liked things being fair.

'Very unusual for the time,' Gran commented, and Tasha nodded again.

'It was. Pirate captains who signed the code didn't have more food or better living conditions than other members of the crew. Many pirates had previously worked as sailors on merchant ships and had been treated terribly. Some poor sailors even died of hunger!'

No wonder they chose to become pirates instead, Lizzie thought. Now that she'd learnt about Sign Hand Stan's fairness towards his fellow pirates, she liked him even more.

'Sign Hand Stan, his crew and the *Stormracer* all mysteriously disappeared one dark and stormy night and were never seen again,' Tasha said. 'Lots of people have looked for the wreck because of the treasure that was supposed to be on board. The *Stormracer* is thought to have sunk somewhere along this coast but no one's ever been able to find it.'

Yet, Lizzie thought to herself – and Lucky looked up at her and wagged her tail. No one had found the *Stormracer* yet, but she and Lucky hadn't been the ones looking for it!

'Can I take pictures of the display on my phone?' Lizzie asked, and Tasha said she could. Lizzie knew Ted was going to be amazed when he saw Sign Hand Stan's portrait and the painting of the *Stormracer*, and even more so when she told him about the pirate code. He'd want to come to the museum and take a look for himself – and no doubt want a cutlass like Tasha's too. Lizzie thought she wouldn't mind a cutlass herself. It could come in very useful when she and Lucky were solving mysteries, and would definitely be good for playing pirates and sword fighting with Ted.

As she was taking a picture of the pirate code, Lizzie realized there was something a good detective should always check. She took her black-light torch from her bag and shone it at the back of the yellowed paper, the bit that wasn't hidden by the easel.

Gran and Tasha leant in close to look too.

They could all see the invisible-ink writing. It showed up as purple under the ultraviolet light of the torch.

Tasha must have known about invisible ink too because her hands flew up to

her face and her mouth made a shocked 'O' shape. Gran made the sign for 'gobsmacked'.

There was definitely

something there, but it was impossible to tell exactly what it was. It could just be marks or a scribble. But there was something!

'We need to be a lot closer and it needs to be darker,' Lizzie signed to her gran.

'You have to be really careful with old paper or you'll accidentally mark it,' warned Tasha, which Gran signed to Lizzie. 'I'd lift it from the easel so we could have a better look, but even though my fingers are clean they might still leave oil traces.'

Lizzie had a solution for that. She pulled her detective gloves from her bag and waved them at Tasha.

Gran's friend looked furtively to her left

and then her right. There didn't seem to be any other visitors in the museum besides Lizzie, Lucky and Gran. Tasha took the gloves from Lizzie, pulled a set of keys from her pocket, unlocked the glass case and carefully lifted the pirate code from the easel.

Lizzie, Lucky and Gran followed her into the cleaning cupboard. It was a bit of a squash with all the mops and brooms, but once Tasha pulled the door closed it was nice and dark.

Lizzie switched on her torch and shone it at the pirate code.

Tasha's gasp made Lucky look up and wag her tail. Lizzie's eyes widened and Gran grasped Lizzie's shoulder.

There was a
SECRET MESSAGE
written on the
BACK OF THE CODE!

CHAPTER 7

Lizzie's heart started to beat very fast as she realized that the message wasn't in writing but little drawings – lots and lots of tiny hands, one after the other, in rows.

'It must be written in a special kind of pirate hieroglyphics,' Tasha said.

Lizzie couldn't lip-read Tasha in the dark, but she could just about make out Gran's signing.

'Is it pirate language?'

Lizzie shook her head. She knew

exactly what this language was, and not only that but she could read it too! It wasn't exactly the same as modern-day sign language, but she remembered what Dad had told her about the vowel signs going in the opposite order in the olden days. Bearing that in mind, the fingerspelling signs shouldn't be too hard to decipher.

Lucky looked up at Lizzie as she pulled a pencil and notebook from her detective bag. If she wrote down the letter each hand was fingerspelling, then she'd be able to read the message.

First of all, though, Lizzie made sure she took a clear photograph of the code on her phone. Then she gave the black-light torch to Gran to shine on the paper so she could write down the letters.

The first one was:

B

The second one:

E

Lizzie held her breath. She was sure Sign Hand Stan had drawn this. Be what, though?

W
A
R
E

Beware.

It said BEWARE!

Lizzie moved on to decipher the next letter.

But at that moment the door suddenly swung open, flooding the cleaning cupboard with light.

Gran dropped the black-light torch on the floor.

Outside stood a furious-looking man with a very red face. 'What are you doing in there?' he shouted.

It wasn't hard for Lizzie to lip-read him. She could even hear him a bit too, he was yelling so loudly.

'I'm sorry,' Tasha said. 'I know it's against the rules, but we've just made an amazing discovery!'

The man didn't let her finish. 'How dare you give a priceless artefact to a little girl to play with!'

Lizzie clenched her fists. She hated being called a little girl!

Lucky looked up at Lizzie fearfully. She could tell the puppy didn't like the angry man – Lizzie didn't like him either.

Lucky picked up the torch from the ground and Lizzie took it from her, putting it back in her detective bag.

'And you've let a *dog* in the museum!' the man yelled.

Tasha held the pirate code out to him and he snatched it from her. He wasn't being careful at all.

'You're FIRED!' he shrieked.

'But, I'm a volunteer,' said Tasha.

'I don't want to see you here ever again – and that applies to you three as well!' the man snapped, pointing at Lizzie, Gran and Lucky.

Lizzie couldn't catch all of what he was saying, but she understood enough to realize who he must be – the new museum owner, Mr Dobson!

'Out! OUT!' he bellowed.

As they left the cupboard, Lizzie saw another man lurking behind one of the exhibits. He was wearing a red baseball cap that he pulled down over his eyes when he saw her looking in his direction. She was *sure* it was the same man she'd spotted earlier on the beach; the one with the Newfoundland dog.

But why was he hiding behind that display? Had he told Mr Dobson where they were? Had he seen Tasha remove the pirate code from its glass case?

They had thought there was nobody else in the museum besides them, but maybe he had been there all the time, spying!

Mr Dobson pointed to the exit and

then just about pushed the four of them
out of it.

'Well, *really*!' Gran said, brushing his
hand away from her arm.

Lizzie lip-read her. She too thought that
Mr Dobson was really, really mean and
unreasonable. They hadn't been doing any
harm – in fact, they'd been helping!

Tasha's shoulders started to shake and
tears flowed down her cheeks.

Gran put her arm round her friend.
'Can you remember the way back to my
house on your own?' she signed quickly to
Lizzie, who nodded.

Tasha was wiping her tears on her
costume sleeve. Lizzie quickly pulled the
packet of tissues from her detective bag
and gave them to her.

'Thank you,' Tasha said.

'I'm sorry you got in trouble,' Lizzie
signed.

Tasha shook her head when Gran
translated. 'It wasn't your fault,' she said,
but she was still crying.

Lizzie thought it probably *was* her fault,
at least a little bit. If she hadn't shown
Tasha that there was something written

on the back of the pirate code, then she wouldn't have taken it out of the display case. But if she'd left it in there, they wouldn't have seen the sign-language drawings. The message was intended to be kept secret – why else would it have been written in invisible ink?

But so far Lizzie had only deciphered one word:

BEWARE.

CHAPTER 8

Lucky danced along beside Lizzie as they headed down the street towards the beach. Inside the Pirate Museum it had been hot, musty and dusty, but outside, the wind was filled with excitement as it ruffled her fur. Lucky liked being outside much better than inside, although it was cooler than before and the sky was now a dark grey.

The tide had been out on their way to the museum and the waves soft and gentle, like they'd just woken up, but now they were wide awake and crashing on the shore.

Lucky and Lizzie ran on to the sand and Lizzie unclipped the little dog's lead.

A gull screeched from above and Lucky raced after it towards the caves, with the cliffs above them. Lucky saw the big dog she'd spotted on the beach earlier in the morning. It was heading down the cliff steps with the man in the red baseball cap. She raced towards the dog, desperate to say hello and have a play.

The big dog looked over at her and wagged its tail, and when Lucky reached him they sniffed hello. Then the Newfoundland gave a woof and a play bow, and the two animals started playing chase.

Their paws kicked up the soft sand as they ran around close to the caves, Lucky's tail wagging with delight.

When the baseball-cap man headed back up the cliff steps, the Newfoundland dog went running after him. But Lucky didn't want to stop playing yet! She chased after her new friend, up the steps that led to the clifftop.

A moment later, Lucky froze in terror at the sound of a loud crash from above. She'd never been out in a proper storm before. A flash of bright

light tore through the sky, followed by
more crashing noises and then heavy rain
beating down all around her.

Lucky ran and ran. Fear filled her so
completely that she could barely breathe,
and she didn't look where she was going.
All she knew was that she had to get
away from the thundering noise and the
silver light that was ripping across the sky.

The gap between the rocks was very
narrow – so narrow that Lucky's
collar was pulled off as she
squeezed her way into
the small dark space.

She breathed a sigh of relief – safe at last . . . only to find her paws scrabbling desperately in the air. She was

falling . . . .

falling!

CHAPTER 9

As she ran after her puppy, Lizzie thought she recognized the big dog Lucky had been playing with. But she wasn't absolutely sure until she saw the man in the red baseball cap coming down the steps of the cliff path above the caves.

It was the same man who'd been on the beach earlier when they'd arrived at Gran and Grandad's house. The one who'd lost the piece of paper with, *missing or stolen*, written on it. The one who'd been hiding behind the exhibit in the museum! How had he got here so quickly? Was he following them?

There was definitely something very suspicious about him, and Lizzie didn't trust him one bit.

She took Lucky's silent dog whistle out of her detective bag but didn't blow on it. Lucky was having such a lovely time playing with the big gentle dog, and the man was still a long way off. A few minutes' play for Lucky couldn't do any harm, and Lizzie wanted a moment to think about the amazing discovery she'd made at the museum.

The invisible-ink drawings had looked almost like ancient Egyptian hieroglyphs and she was desperate to know what the rest of the sign-language message said. She pulled out her phone to look at the photograph she'd taken.

Could Sign Hand Stan really have written it?

If only they hadn't been interrupted by Mr Dobson she could have deciphered more of it. Then she thought about poor Tasha. She'd been so upset.

Glancing up from her phone, Lizzie saw the puppy start chasing after the Newfoundland dog across the sand beyond the caves. They were running towards the man in the baseball cap, who was heading back up the cliff-path steps.

Lizzie blew on the dog whistle but Lucky was too far away and the wind was blowing in the wrong direction, so she didn't come running back like she usually did. The steps went all the way to the clifftop above the caves.

Lizzie ran across the sand and raced up the steps after Lucky, frantically blowing the whistle. The wind coming in off the sea grew stronger, and the sand whipped around and stung her face and eyes.

A flash of lightning ripped through the dark sky.

One second Lizzie could see the puppy running ahead of her and the next she was gone. **Completely gone!**

Lizzie's heart started pounding with fear. Where was Lucky? She kept blowing the dog whistle over and over as she hurried on in the direction she'd last seen her.

The thunder was so loud it shuddered through Lizzie and, a moment later, there was more lightning and then torrential rain.

Lizzie's stomach was in knots of fear. Could the man in the baseball cap have stolen her? Was that why Lucky had disappeared so suddenly?

Lucky had been stolen before when she was just a tiny pup and Lizzie had rescued her. She was determined to find Lucky again now and she wouldn't give up until she had.

Lizzie looked all around her but she couldn't see any sign of Lucky. It was hard to see anything through the heavy rain.

In no time at all Lizzie was soaked through but she wouldn't leave the clifftop, not without Lucky.

She searched and searched, feeling more and more desperate, when through her tears and the rain she spotted Lucky's collar on the ground, half hidden by a rock. She ran over and picked it up.

But where was Lucky?

Lizzie knew that when dogs were scared they sometimes liked to find a small dark place to hide in, like a den.

Lizzie pressed her face to the narrow gap between the rocks. She wasn't completely sure but she thought she could just hear Lucky faintly barking from somewhere inside – not stolen but trapped! Lucky must have been very scared by the storm, and the narrow gap in the rocks might have seemed like a good place to hide.

The gap was very small, too narrow for a grown-up to squeeze through, but not too small for Lizzie.

Lizzie bit her bottom lip. She had to help Lucky, but she was worried about getting trapped in the small space too. She pressed the connect button on her phone to let Mum and Dad know where she was but there was no phone reception. The storm was blocking the signal. Lizzie sighed. A good detective needed to plan ahead and look at problems from every angle. If she got trapped with Lucky, that wouldn't solve anything or help anyone – and no one would know where they were.

But then Lizzie had an idea. She'd leave a note along with Lucky's collar, close to the gap in the rocks where they'd be easy to find. If she weighed it down with her magnifying glass, it wouldn't blow away or get wet! She pulled the magnifying glass, her notebook and pencil from her detective bag.

Lizzie and Lucky are in here ⟶

Then she carefully squeezed her way between the rocks. With her detective bag pushed to the side, her hands feeling the cold dampness of the rocky ground and her knees getting scraped, she moved slowly forward into the darkness.

She could hear Lucky barking faintly, over and over in the distance. But she couldn't tell where the puppy was or which direction the barks were coming from. As Lizzie edged gingerly onwards along the cold stone, all she could hope was that the puppy wasn't injured.

But a moment later there was nothing for her hands to press down on – just space! The rock ledge must have given way, maybe a long time ago when the landslide happened.

Fortunately, she'd been travelling slowly and could ease herself backwards. She didn't know how big the gap was, but how was she going to reach Lucky now? Lucky must have fallen into the space, but just how far had she fallen?

Lizzie pulled the torch from her bag and switched it to the white-light setting. She could see a puppy-shaped shadow five metres below. As soon as Lucky saw her she started running back and forth, barking. Not badly hurt at all!

Lizzie shone her torch at the gap ahead of her. It was too wide to cross, but there was something white hovering close to the space. For a second Lizzie couldn't breathe. **It looked like a ghost** – a cave ghost with arms outstretched, almost close enough to touch!

Lucky gave a louder bark and Lizzie swung the torch down towards her and then gasped. Next to Lucky were more ghosts – lots of them floating upwards. But wait, no – they weren't ghosts after all, Lizzie realized. They were the canvas sails of an ancient ship, and next to each one of them hung a rope that sailors would have used to let the sails up and down.

Lizzie shone her torch around and saw more sails and ropes going up and up. Maybe the canvas sails below had helped to break Lucky's fall. The puppy was on the wooden deck of a ship close to the wheel. But what was a ship doing inside a cave?

The nearest sail and rope were so close that Lizzie could almost touch them if she stretched out far enough. Almost but not quite; not without the risk of falling – and

a five-metre fall could hurt a lot. Getting injured wouldn't help her or Lucky.

Then Lizzie remembered the folding umbrella with the hook-shaped handle that Gran had given her in case it rained. It was still in her bag. She took the umbrella out, opening the telescopic handle as far as it would go. Now she could easily reach the rope and bring it towards her. Then, having tested its strength with a powerful tug, Lizzie made her way down to Lucky.

The puppy was so excited to be rescued that she licked and licked her, and Lizzie hugged the puppy and kissed her furry head. The two of them were uninjured and together again!

Lizzie gazed at the ledge above. She could just see a tiny beam of light shining through the narrow gap, but they couldn't get back out that way. Lucky couldn't climb a rope and she'd be too heavy for Lizzie to carry while climbing.

How were they going to get out? How would anyone know where they were?

Lizzie gave herself a little shake. She wasn't going to think about that. She was very glad she'd brought her detective bag with her, and Gran's umbrella had come in very useful indeed!

Lizzie pulled her torch from her bag and switched it on. She knew she had to find a solution to their problem and she was determined to get Lucky out of the cave, home and safe.

Lucky licked Lizzie's hand and Lizzie stroked her.

She wouldn't let her puppy down.

CHAPTER 10

Lizzie and Lucky stepped carefully along the wooden deck, avoiding the holes where falling rocks had damaged the old ship. Lucky's night vision was much better than Lizzie's, but she stayed close anyway because she didn't want to be separated from her again. Every now and then Lizzie saw Lucky look up at the gap high above them and give a bark.

When they reached the bow of the vessel, Lizzie gasped. She knew exactly who this ship had once belonged to!

The figurehead at the front wasn't a king, a queen, a dragon or a unicorn. It was a giant carved wooden hand holding a box with a padlock on it.

Lizzie's heart started thumping very fast – they'd found the *Stormracer*, Sign Hand Stan's ship, and if the box was what she thought it was . . . then they'd found some pirate treasure!

She knew there was no phone reception in the cave but the camera still worked. Remembering to act like a good detective even in the midst of her excitement, Lizzie took some pictures and a video as evidence.

Close to the ship's wheel there were wooden steps leading downwards, so Lizzie went to explore as Lucky trotted after her.

In the main cabin there was a large wooden table with chairs round it. There were even a few metal plates and beakers set out on the table.

Lucky tasted a few crumbs lying on the floor. Not bad – not as nice as her puppy biscuits, but still hard.

In the very centre of the table, under

a small wooden box with the letter 'S' on it, was a ship's logbook. Lizzie shone her torch on the last entry so she could read what it said.

The King's men are after us and the penalty for piracy is death. Tonight, under cover of the moon, we will flee in all directions of the kingdom, never set sail again and be pirates no more . . .

Lizzie picked up the wooden box and looked inside. It contained a sharp flint stone and some dry cloth. She realized it must be a tinderbox that held the materials for lighting a fire.

There was more writing roughly carved
inside the box's lid:

*Do not look up to the sky for
freedom when the way is down.*

Lizzie frowned. Was Sign Hand Stan
telling them about another way to get out?
In the mystery stories she read there was
sometimes a trapdoor under the rug . . .
and there was a rug in this room too!

Lizzie lifted up a corner of the rug
and gasped when she saw there was
indeed a square door with

a metal pull set into the wooden floor.

She opened the trapdoor to reveal more steps going downwards.

Taking her detective notebook and pencil from her bag, Lizzie decided it was time to make a map.

After the steps there was a narrow tunnel that Lizzie added to her map as she and Lucky moved cautiously down it. The tunnel was very dark but Lizzie had her torch and night-vision binoculars, and Lucky trotted on ahead of her.

The end of the tunnel was blocked, but Lucky found another pathway to the right. Lizzie made a note of it on her map. She had to bend down to get into this passage but within a few metres she could stand up again. **More cave puzzles!**

They went to the left and were in another tunnel that Lizzie added to her map, but it was also blocked and they had to turn again. Lizzie noted it all down as they walked on and on in the dark.

It felt like they'd been walking for hours.

Lucky sat down and started panting. Lizzie frowned as she looked about them, sure that they'd come this way already.

It was hard to tell, though, as the cave walls looked very similar. But as she stared up at the stalactites, Lizzie was certain the pattern they made was familiar. She added the stalactites, to her map and picked up some pebbles, arranging three of them in a triangle shape. Now she'd be able to tell if they came back this way and were going round in circles.

From then on, whichever route they tried, Lizzie kept putting down three pebbles in the triangle shape as a marker so she'd know where they'd been.

A short while later, Lucky gave a wag of her tail and Lizzie breathed a big sigh of relief. No need for the night-vision binoculars or torch any more.

Ahead of them, in the distance, there was a speck of bright sunlight.

CHAPTER 11

Lizzie and Lucky blinked as they came out on to the beach through one of the smaller caves, not far from the one with the huge boulder in front of it.

The storm was over and the sun was shining again, although it was still spitting with rain. Far out to sea, on the horizon, Lizzie could see the faded outline of a rainbow.

Lucky was so delighted to be in the daylight again that she danced around in circles and Lizzie laughed and laughed. They were free and unhurt and had made the most amazing discovery! The two of them raced back across the beach to Gran and Grandad's house.

In all the excitement, Lizzie was a bit surprised by all the worried faces that greeted them when they burst in through

the front door. Mum, Dad, Gran, Grandad and Ted were all in a total panic.

'Where were you?' signed Dad.

'We've been so worried!' signed Mum.

'I thought you'd come straight back here after the museum,' said Gran.

'Why didn't you text us?' signed Mum.

'We called the police,' signed Dad.

Mum and Dad hugged Lizzie to them tightly.

'Thank goodness you're safe!' they both signed. But then they started to worry about the state she was in instead.

'You're soaked through,' signed Mum.

'Are you hurt?' signed Dad.

'Where were you?' Grandad asked.

'Why are your clothes torn?' Mum signed.

'What happened to you?' Gran said.

'We found it!' Lizzie signed, when she could finally get a word in.

But her family and friend only looked confused, and not excited as she'd expected. Lucky lay down on the carpet and went to sleep. She was exhausted after all her adventures.

'We found Sign Hand Stan's ship! The *Stormracer*! It had a treasure chest . . . I took a video and some pictures.' Lizzie took out her phone to show them.

Although they weren't the clearest pictures or video in the world, it was easy to see that she and Lucky had discovered something.

'If it wasn't for Lucky I'd never have found it. It's Sign Hand Stan's ship – the whole ship! It's inside a cave and there are tunnels – we got a bit lost for a while, but look! There's the treasure chest.'

'You're our treasure,' signed Dad. 'Not metal and stones.'

'You could have been hurt. We didn't

know where you were. You could have been trapped in the cave . . . with the tide coming in,' Mum signed and a tear slipped down her face, followed by another and another.

Lizzie rubbed her fist in a small circle close to her left shoulder to sign that she was sorry. She really hadn't meant to scare them at all.

Mum and Dad hugged her even more tightly then.

'Looks like a box in a fist,' Dad signed at last, pointing to the photo of the figurehead and treasure chest she'd taken.

Lizzie nodded. She couldn't wait for them to open the treasure chest and see exactly what was inside it. 'Come on, I'll show you,' she signed.

'No, you get changed into some warm clothes first,' Mum told her.

'But the treasure . . . and there's a logbook too. Sign Hand Stan's diary!'

Mum and Dad shook their heads.

'First things first – we don't want you getting ill,' signed Mum.

'We want you safe,' Dad signed.

'The tide's coming in now anyway,' Grandad said. 'Those caves will be cut off in no time. No one's going inside them for a while.'

Dad was busy video-signing on his phone, informing the police sign-language interpreter that Lizzie had been found and the search party could be called off.

'How long until the tide goes out?' Ted wanted to know, as Lizzie lip-read intently. She really, *really* wanted to show them Sign Hand Stan's ship.

'It'll be a few hours yet,' Grandad said, looking through the window. So Lizzie went upstairs to have a shower and change into some dry clothes.

★

'Still can't go exploring the caves yet,' said Grandad, when Lizzie came back down again a little while later.

Lucky yawned, stretched and opened her eyes. She'd been having a lovely sleep while Lizzie was busy.

'So we might as well eat,' said Gran, who was pottering around putting some home-made tomato soup, bread, seaweed chutney, pickles and salad on the table.

Lizzie took a plate of fruit outside for Iggy and Boo, and Lucky followed her out into the back garden.

'Woof, WOOF, woof!'

Boo squawked as soon as he saw Lucky.

'I tried to teach Boo some more words, but he likes "woof" best,' Ted said.

Lucky still wasn't too sure about Gran and Grandad's pets. She gave a quick wag of her tail but didn't bark back at the parrot.

★

Even after everyone had eaten, the tide still hadn't gone out far enough to allow any exploration of the caves.

Lizzie and Ted looked at the photos she'd taken on her phone, and Ted helped her to decipher the rest of the message on the back of the pirate code:

BEWARE THE KING'S MEN.

Neither of them knew who the King's men were.

'Got your old metal detector working again,' Grandad told Dad, holding up the metal stick. 'All it needed was a new battery, even after all these years. Found your old pram too and fixed that up in the workshop. Just needed a bit of welding to adjust the wheel.'

Lucky sniffed at the small blue baby pram on the carpet.

'Didn't use that metal detector much after Max and I stopped being friends,' Dad signed sadly.

Grandad switched the metal detector on and gave it to Lizzie as Gran sprinkled some spare change across the wooden floor.

'Sweep it across the ground, but not too quickly,' Dad told Lizzie.

The metal detector's light flashed whenever she swept it over a coin.

'Me next,' said Ted eagerly, and he swept it across the floor and found more coins.

'Not long before we can go to the caves now,' Grandad said, checking the state of the tide through the window, and Lizzie held up both thumbs.

'Where's Lucky?' she signed, looking around for the puppy. Her breath caught in her chest and suddenly it was hard to breathe. Lucky had been there just a moment before, but now she was gone. Lizzie couldn't lose her twice in one day!

Mum touched Lizzie on the shoulder and pointed at Dad's old pram.

Lucky was lying in it, curled up and fast asleep.

'Looks nice and comfy,' signed Dad as the puppy snoozed.

Lizzie breathed a sigh of relief, grinned and nodded. Lucky looked very comfortable indeed.

★

'Better get ready, then,' Grandad said, looking out of the window at the beach and the caves beyond. The tide was almost out.

Before they left, they collected as many torches as they could find.

'I'm taking this, just in case,' Grandad said, picking up a coil of rope.

Ted wore a head torch and Gran carried a camping lantern. They were ready!

★

Lizzie, Mum, Dad, Gran, Grandad and Ted headed across the beach to the caves. Lucky was wide awake now and delighted to be going out for another play on the sand. She followed everyone else into the cave from which she and Lizzie had recently escaped.

Lizzie held the map she'd made, and led the way confidently. She reckoned that the big cave with the boulder in front of it was probably where Sign Hand Stan's ship was really hidden. Maybe it had been blocked off by the landslide, or maybe the pirate crew had pushed the boulder there on purpose. They couldn't have known the same large rock would still be in place hundreds of years later!

Everyone followed Lizzie into the smaller cave that led to Sign Hand Stan's ship. It looked as though there wasn't anywhere to go at the end of it, but now Lizzie and Lucky knew about the small, hidden side route.

It was a real squeeze for the grown-ups, especially Dad, but they managed.

'We can always use my rope to pull you if need be,' Grandad joked, holding up the coil he'd brought with him.

Lizzie led them onward through the twists and turns, past the three-pebble clues and stalactites, until they reached the lower deck of the *Stormracer* and went up the steps.

'This way,' she beckoned, her night-vision binoculars round her neck and her torch lighting the path ahead. But as she looked up at the *Stormracer*'s giant hand figurehead her mouth fell open.

The treasure chest had gone!

Who could have taken it? Where could it be? How could someone have got into the cave when the tide was in?

'It was right there!' she signed, pointing at the now-empty carved wooden hand.

Someone had **STOLEN** the pirate **TREASURE!**

CHAPTER 12

As they came out of the cave, Lucky suddenly started to wag her tail excitedly. Lizzie followed the puppy's gaze just in time to spot the man in the red baseball cap and his dog coming out of another cave close by. He was carrying what looked like a square box – *or a pirate's treasure chest* – wrapped in part of a canvas sail.

The Newfoundland dog began to dig in the sand and a moment later Lucky was there, joining in. She loved digging!

Lizzie pointed towards the man and signed **'Thief!'** to her dad, then started running after the robber.

Dad, Mum, Ted, Gran and Grandad raced after Lizzie, and when the man realized he was being chased, he started running as well. Then the two dogs joined in the game!

But Lizzie's dad played rugby for the national Deaf team, so he caught up with the thief in no time and tackled him. The man dropped the box and Lizzie could see that it really was Sign Hand Stan's treasure chest.

'It was you!' Lizzie signed. '*You stole Sign Hand Stan's treasure!*'

Dad stared at the man. 'Max?' he signed. 'Is it you?'

The man struggled to get away but Dad was too strong. Finally he gave up and nodded.

'Your childhood friend Max is the thief?' signed Lizzie.

The Newfoundland jumped on top of him.

'It's not a game, Beast,' Max told the big dog when it started licking his face. 'I'm not a criminal, not really,' Max signed to Lizzie. He used a mixture of sign language and speech, like Gran and Grandad did. 'I was saving the treasure from a *real* thief.'

Now Lizzie was confused. 'Saving it?'

'Yes – from Edward Dobson. He's been buying up all these small local museums and then selling off any valuable items from them and keeping the money himself. It's a crime and he's getting away with it! Once he knows about Sign Hand Stan's ship, he'll be all over it like a fly on honey. There's gold still on board the ship, lots of it. Too much for me to carry, although I've got a few coins in here. But I couldn't let him take this . . .'

Max opened the chest and pulled out a square woodcut with drawings of hands on it – similar to the invisible-ink hands on the back of the pirate code.

'I knew there was a risk that people, especially greedy people, might not realize the incredible emotional value of this.'

'What is it?'

Lizzie's mum squeezed her shoulder

and Lizzie looked up
at her. Mum's eyes
opened very
wide, like she'd
seen something
she couldn't quite
believe.

'A sign-language alphabet woodcut.
Maybe even older than the *Digiti-Lingua*
of sixteen ninety-eight.'

'The *Digiti*-what?' Ted asked.

'The first time a record of the two-
handed British sign language we use
today was published was in a thirty-page
pamphlet called the *Digiti-Lingua*,' Max
explained. 'No one knows who the author
was as it was written anonymously.'

'This is priceless to the sign-language community,' Mum signed as she looked at the beautiful woodcut. A tear ran down her face as she smiled. 'So little of our history has been kept. An artefact like this must be shared, not hidden away or sold to an individual highest bidder. It's worth far more than any amount of money.'

Max nodded. 'I know. That's why I took it. Not to steal but to keep it safe.' He turned to Lizzie. 'I followed you, or rather Beast followed you. We were walking along when suddenly he raced off. It was as if he heard you calling . . .'

Lizzie nodded because she knew exactly what Beast had heard. She showed Max the silent dog whistle and he made the sign for 'Now I get it'.

'I saw the note you left but Beast and I were both far too big to go in after you, and even though I called and Beast barked, you didn't come back,' Max said. 'Although we heard your puppy barking.'

Then it was Lizzie's turn to make the sign for 'Now I understand'. She told Max that Lucky had been barking but she hadn't known why. Lucky must have heard Beast and Max!

'I kept calling and calling. We were just heading down the cliff steps to your grandparents' house to tell them where you were and about the note you'd left, when we saw you and your puppy coming out of one of the caves on the beach. When you went running across the sand I realized you didn't need our help after all. But Beast went running into the cave you'd come out of and I went after him. We couldn't get out again until the tide had gone down. But in the meantime we came across the *Stormracer* – just like you had already done before us. We'd never have found it without you – I followed your clues.'

Dad looked at Max for a moment before patting his former companion on the shoulder. 'Glad to have my old friend back,' he signed. And before Max could protest, Dad wrapped him in a big bear hug. Beast gave Dad a lick and Lucky did the same.

'But we can't just keep the alphabet

woodcut,' Lizzie signed. 'That would be wrong too.'

'Sign Hand Stan said he wanted it to go to the Deaf community, along with all his treasure. It was written in his log,' Max said. He held up the book Lizzie had seen on the table.

'Maybe the woodcut could go somewhere like the Sign Language Museum?' Dad signed.

'That would be perfect,' signed Mum, and Lizzie agreed. Then anyone who wanted to could see it and also learn more about the mystery of Sign Hand Stan.

CHAPTER 13

'We need to catch Dobson in the act of trying to steal an artefact,' Max signed when they'd got back to Gran and Grandad's house.

While he was talking, Lizzie and Ted inspected the coins from the bottom of the treasure chest. Some of them were still golden, but others were black.

Lizzie frowned and signed 'Why?'

'The ones that have turned black are made from silver,' Grandad explained.

'The blackness proves that they are real silver.'

Dad nodded and Lizzie made the sign for **'WOW'** – she hadn't known that before.

'There's hundreds of coins like this still on board the ship?' Ted asked.

'Maybe thousands,' Max told him. 'Catching Dobson in the act of stealing is the only way to stop him. Otherwise, in his position as museum owner, he'd just deny it and people would believe him. We think he's been selling items anonymously online. Yesterday, an emerald flag holder was identified as coming from the Pirate Museum. That's when I was called in. There are millions of stolen artefacts out there, depriving countries of what's rightfully theirs and robbing people of their history and heritage.'

Lizzie nodded. They needed to think of a way of tricking the new museum owner into revealing himself as a thief.

'But how could we catch him in the act?' Ted asked, scratching his head.

Lizzie had already thought of a way. 'We give him something to steal and try to sell. Something that looks too valuable to resist!'

'Not Sign Hand Stan's woodcut alphabet!' signed Mum.

Lizzie shook her head. 'That's far too amazing and precious to allow anywhere near Mr Dobson. We need something fake that *looks* real.'

She glanced over at her mum and dad and grinned. She knew just the thing. 'A fake jewel. A big one. But it has to look expensive and real and feel heavy and be a bit battered or maybe muddy. Caked-on mud would be good.'

Mum and Dad had experience making fake jewels. They'd made lots for Princess Joanna's crown. Now all they had to do was trick Mr Dobson with one of them. The museum owner, however, was unlikely to be deceived by a prop. This one had to be more professional. Rubies were almost as hard as diamonds. They'd need a lot of heat – and fortunately Gran and Grandad's clay oven and welding equipment would come in very useful.

It was nearly closing time, but Mum and Dad could just about make it to the shops to buy what they needed to make the ruby before they shut.

'You'll have to take the fake jewel into the museum. Mr Dobson won't suspect you,' Lizzie signed to Ted.

'You could say you found it when you were treasure hunting on the beach,' Grandad told him, holding up the metal detector. 'A prop's always useful

151

as a distraction. Maybe take one of the blackened silver coins too.'

Ted wondered if he should wear a disguise but everyone agreed he would be better just looking like himself. Hiding in plain sight.

'You'd easily pass as a beachcomber,' Gran told him.

★

As soon as Mum and Dad got back from the shops they set to work making a fake ruby. Tasha was let in on the secret and agreed to help. She got in touch with the Arts and Antiquities Unit of the police

so they'd be ready to take action when
needed. They'd worked with Max a few
years ago when he'd been involved in
returning stolen items to the original
countries from which they'd been taken.

A police guard was set up to watch
over the *Stormracer* and the treasure still
on board. Not that Lizzie believed
anyone could have found the
ship – it was amazing that Lucky
had done so by accident. The
Stormracer had remained hidden for
hundreds of years, and probably would
have remained undiscovered for many
more, if it hadn't been for Lucky.

★

When Lizzie got up the next morning the

153

ruby looked perfect to her. Large enough
to entice Mr Dobson, but not so large that
it was obviously fake. It was covered in
caked-on mud but there was enough of
the gem visible to recognize it as a ruby.
She didn't know how well-informed Mr
Dobson was about jewels but she knew he
was greedy, so she hoped that would be
enough to convince him this was the real
thing. Once he tried to sell it he could be
arrested and charged.

'We'll come with you – as your
bodyguards,' Lizzie's mum and dad signed
to Ted.

'I don't need bodyguards,' Ted signed
back.

Dad shook his head and winked at

him. 'We also want to see if we can trick Dobson with our home-made ruby,' he signed.

Ted nodded.

Lizzie really, really wanted to go to the museum too, but she didn't want to leave Lucky behind – and it would be hard to disguise the puppy. She looked over at Lucky snoozing in Dad's old pram again and had a thought. Maybe it wouldn't be so hard to disguise her after all!

'Max brought your magnifying glass back and left this for you late last night,' Dad signed. 'He said you might find it useful.'

Lizzie's eyes opened very wide. Max was right! She stared at the tiny spy camera in her hand. It was just what every good detective needed.

Ted grinned, and after breakfast the two of them set it up together. Now Lizzie would be able to watch Ted's meeting with Mr Dobson on her phone.

They were ready.

Mum and Dad left first so they'd be in the museum when Ted arrived. Lizzie had suggested it would look suspicious if everyone turned up at the same time and they had agreed she was right.

Lucky stayed in Dad's old pram, pushed by Lizzie, all the way to the museum. Ted had the ruby and the metal detector, and Mum and Dad took up their positions as museum visitors.

As Ted headed through the door with the fake ruby, Lizzie pulled out her phone and tuned in to the spy camera.

Mr Dobson was very interested indeed as Ted told him he'd found a strange red rock on the beach when he'd been

157

metal-detecting, and especially when he showed him the ancient coin that he'd discovered lying next to it. Ted gave Mr Dobson the ruby that Mum and Dad had made. It was as heavy as the real thing.

'I'll need to get this authenticated,' Mr Dobson told Ted. 'I'll ask one of my staff to take a look.'

'OK,' Ted agreed. 'Should I have a receipt?'

'Oh no, you don't need anything like that. You can trust me. We'll shake on it.' Mr Dobson shook hands with Ted. 'I'll let you know when it's been assessed.'

Ted came running out to join Lizzie and Lucky. He held both thumbs up and signed **'Perfect!'**

It had all gone exactly as Lizzie had planned. None of them believed for a moment that Mr Dobson had any intention of getting the ruby properly checked out. He was too greedy for that!

Lizzie's phone flashed as Mum and Dad left the museum too. Max had texted to say Dobson had already put the ruby up for sale online.

Lizzie had only just read his text when she received another one. The fake ruby had sold and the buyer was on their way to collect it! Lizzie texted Max back.

Is it usually this fast?

Sometimes. He must have had a particular buyer in mind – one he knew was looking for shipwreck artefacts. I'll be there in a minute.

Lizzie, Lucky, Mum, Dad, Ted and Max kept an eye on the entrance to the museum from their hiding place. The Arts and Antiquities Unit were hidden in a fake ice-cream van. Lizzie thought it was a very good disguise – unless someone wanted to buy an ice cream!

A few minutes later a limousine drove up and stopped in front of the museum. Mr Dobson must have been expecting it because he came running down the steps.

Lizzie watched as the car window glided down and Mr Dobson handed over a velvet black bag. She was sure it must have the ruby inside.

The Arts and Antiquities Unit must have thought so too because they all jumped out of the front, back and middle of the ice-cream van and quickly surrounded Mr Dobson and the limousine.

Lizzie could tell that Mr Dobson was very angry. He was shouting and shaking his fists, but she could only manage to lip-read the words, 'Don't you know who I am?'

'He's telling the police that they can't

arrest him because he's rich and a very important person,' Ted signed.

But the police didn't care about that. One of the officers arrested Mr Dobson while another radioed for backup. Two police cars arrived soon afterwards and a few seconds later, Mr Dobson was sitting in the back of the first vehicle. The man

and woman who'd bought the ruby were put in the back of the second one. They looked just as angry as Mr Dobson.

'Those two are notorious for buying up stolen artefacts as well – and selling them on at an even higher price,' Max told Lizzie.

Lizzie signed that they didn't look like criminals.

'That's the problem,' Max signed back. 'You can't always tell whether a person's good or bad just by looking at them.'

Lizzie nodded. She had thought Max was bad at first, but he turned out to be a good person in the end.

She and Ted high-fived as the criminals were taken away, and Lucky wagged her tail and jumped out of the pram. It was time to go to the beach and enjoy the rest of their holiday.

CHAPTER 14

In the evening Gran, Grandad, Mum, Dad, Ted, Lizzie and Lucky had a celebration barbecue on the beach.

Tasha came to join them. She'd been put in charge of the museum and there was no risk of it being closed any more. 'The Pirate Museum is famous!' she said happily.

The story of Lizzie and Lucky finding the *Stormracer* and hundreds of gold coins on board, as well as the sign-language alphabet woodcut, had been on the evening news. The fact that the former museum owner, Mr Dobson, had been a thief who robbed small museums while pretending to help them had made the story even more newsworthy.

★

Lucky was very pleased to see Beast when he and Max joined them all for the barbecue on the beach. The two dogs dug and dug and dug. They sent sand flying up into the air and over everyone with their speedy paws.

'Careful, you two!' said Grandad, but the dogs were having too much fun to take any notice. Every now and then they'd look over at each other, give a wag of their tails and continue digging.

'They'll probably find more treasure if they keep on digging like that,' laughed Ted. Boo was perched on his shoulder and encouraged the dogs with an occasional **'Woof!'**

At last Beast decided he'd had enough of digging in the sand, so he lay on his

back, waggling his legs in the air and rolling around as if he had an itch that needed scratching. Lucky watched him for a second and then she rolled on to her back and copied him. Sand-rolling was almost (but not quite) as much fun as digging. It was very good when you needed a rest, though.

'Woof, **woof**, woof,'

barked Boo the parrot, and Beast jumped in surprise.

*

Lizzie kept thinking about what she'd read in Sign Hand Stan's logbook.

The King's men are after us and the penalty for piracy is death. Tonight under cover of the moon we will flee in all directions of the kingdom, never set sail again and be pirates no more . . .

'Who were the King's men?' she signed to Max.

'Pirate hunters who worked for the King,' he signed back.

'So what happened to Sign Hand Stan?' Lizzie signed. She hoped he hadn't been caught by the royal hunters.

Max shook his head. 'We don't know.'

Lizzie looked at Dad. He shook his head too.

'But we *do* know he wasn't caught,' Max continued. 'There's a list of all the pirates who were captured and there's no record of Sign Hand Stan or any of his crew. All we know is that the *Stormracer* was hidden in the cave and Sign Hand Stan and his men disappeared.'

'One dark and stormy night,' signed Dad.

'So he survived?' Lizzie signed with a smile.

'I hope so,' said Max, crossing his fingers.

'Me too,' signed Dad.

'I wonder what he did afterwards?' Lizzie signed. 'What his life was like?'

'Maybe he went on to be a farmer, or a teacher – he could have been anything at all. Maybe he didn't even need to work because of all the money he'd made during his pirating years,' Ted said.

'Woof, woof,' Boo agreed.

'Sign Hand Stan painted a picture of the *Stormracer*, remember? He could have become an artist,' Lizzie signed.

'Or a prop maker and jewel forger like

me and your mum,' signed Dad, and they all laughed.

Lizzie was very glad that Sign Hand Stan's most treasured possession, the alphabet woodcut, was on its way to the Sign Language Museum, where it would have pride of place, just as the pirate would have wished.

Lucky went into the house and came back with her yellow octopus toy. She dropped it next to Beast and looked up at him with a wag of her tail.

As it grew colder, Lizzie and Lucky huddled together under a blanket and gazed at the moon and the stars.

'Pirates used to steer their boats by looking up at the stars,' Gran said, 'but nowadays we don't need to – we'd have a map of the sea on our phones.'

Lizzie stroked Lucky's furry head and imagined the two of them setting out on a pirate ship with a skull-and-crossbones flag on a stormy, moonlit sea.

Tasha brought out a home-made cake decorated with a treasure map, then Grandad lit a bonfire and they toasted marshmallows in the flames on extra-long forks that he'd made in his workshop.

Dad and Mum danced along to pirate-movie music that Dad played at absolute full volume so they could hear and feel it, and no one complained about the noise.

Boo stayed perched on Ted's shoulder like a true pirate's parrot.

'I wish I could have met Sign Hand Stan,' Lizzie signed.

'And I bet he wishes he could have met you and Lucky,' Ted signed back. 'The mystery of the stolen treasure would never have been solved if it hadn't been for your amazing detective skills.'

Lucky looked up at Lizzie and wagged her tail.

Lizzie hugged Lucky to her and wondered what their next mystery would be.

THE END

LEARN TO SIGN

Can you read the dedication at the front of the book using sign language?

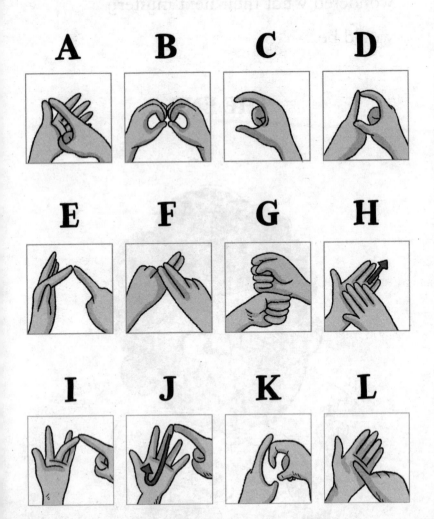

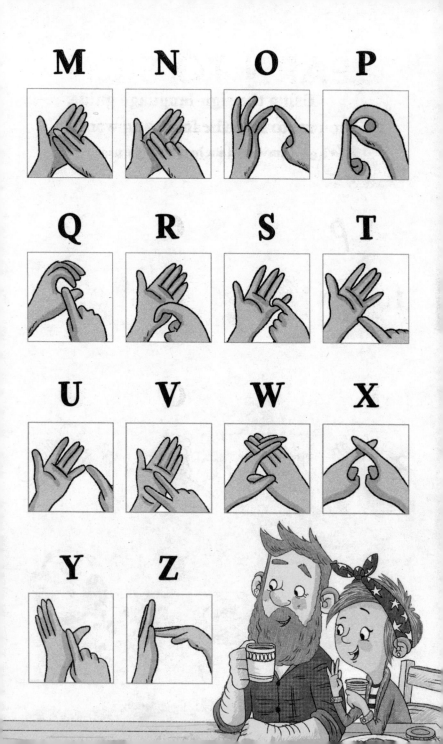

Using the sign-language guide, try to sign the following words:
(Answers at the bottom of the page.)

1 ρ

2

3

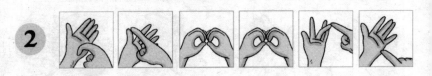

4

....

5

....

6

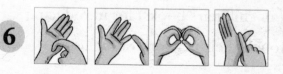

AHOY THERE!

I love writing about pirates – almost as much as I love creating mysteries for Lizzie and Lucky to solve.

The brilliant crew of *The Mystery of the Missing Treasure* included:

Tim Budgen and his amazing art work, plus designers Arabella Jones and Mandy Norman. And thanks to Inclusive Minds (the CIC supporting and championing inclusion and diversity in children's books) for introducing us to Gift through their network of Inclusion Ambassadors.

On the editorial wheel-deck: the totally brilliant editors, Sara Jafari and Emma Jones. Copy-editors Mary O'Riordon and Stephanie Barrett with sea cats, Pretzel and Flapjack.

Proofreaders Leah Boulton and Pippa Noble, who knows sign language too. Plus my lovely agent and navigator Clare Pearson.

Fantastic publicist, Phoebe Williams, and marketer, Michelle Nathan, as well as Rozzie Todd, Toni Budden and Kat Baker who all worked so hard on the sales – thank you very much.

As my sign language has improved, my signing friends have increased. My BSL sign language tutor, Jagjeet Rose, knows all the sea signs I could ask for, plus lots of hilarious sign language jokes. Thank you, Jagjeet.

Most of the story is made up, of course, but Princess Joanna of Scotland was real and so is the Digiti-Lingua. Thank you to sign language historian Peter R Brown for answering my history questions.

My story-inspiring golden retrievers, Freya and Ellie, both love the beach and we go there whenever we can so they can dig in the sand, swim in the sea and make new dog friends.

My husband, Eric, also loves the seaside and it's not surprising to find him singing as he makes breakfast in the early hours of the morning. We all bundle into the car, often when it's still dark, and arrive when the tide's just right, and we have the empty beach to ourselves. So far we haven't spotted any pirate ships – but you never know. I love my new turquoise turtle and mermaid hearing-aid bling.

Thanks to everyone who inspired, shared information and helped to create this book. But, most all, thanks to 'the captain' for whom this book was written! Our reader. You.

MAY YOUR SHIP ALWAYS SAIL TRUE.

Megan